ikizukuri

Clusters of people dominate the streets,

Dashing left, dashing right, from all directions

Yet their expression remained masked by their historic customs.

Struggling to keep up with the dynamic rhythm,

You find solace in an obscure restaurant,

Parting the flailing curtains with your clammy hands as you enter,

Blissfully unaware of the malignity you would face.

'Table for one,' you demand,

The deep sound resonates across the sparsely lit room

As the waitress politely guides you towards the bar,

Face to face with the infamous 'chef'.

Overwhelmed by the choices on the menu,

You turn to the 'chef' for his advice

'Take your pick', he replies as he directs his line
of vision towards the tank.

You lean closer,

The pungent scent of fish travels up your nose

Lingering heavily in the humid air,

As you carefully select the next victim.

After closely examining each specimen,

You take a risk

Then the 'chef' plunges his hand into the tank

Grabbing the octopus by its tentacles

It frantically wriggles itself creating bubbles that
rise to the surface

Nevertheless, the monotonous 'chef' lifted it out

While the octopus gasped for its last breath,

The froth at the surface simmered down

As if the octopus' efforts were futile.

The vulnerable, slimy victim lay on the wooden board

Pathetically wriggling and slapping its tentacles

yearning to return home

away from this unknown territory

For it longed to regain control of its fate.

The 'chef' began the procedure by inspecting it,

Pressing his hands against the smooth, slippery flesh

Making sure that he was familiar with the location of each organ.

Then he draws up a knife

With a blade so polished that it obscured all the lives that it took,

As he Meticulously slices through its skin,

His unwavering focus rendered him successful

For now, the octopus was prepared alive

A forlorn silence filled the room as if to honour its life.

You stare blankly at the dish in front of you,

It seems that this won't be the last time such a 'delicacy' is served

So, you bring yourself to take a reluctant bite,

hoping that the freshness will distract you from the guilt, shame and disgust

but it's impossible

what was once a freshness in your mouth transfigured into a bitter resentment

yet when you realise this it's too late.

wriggle, wriggle, wriggle...

Broken Shells

A burdensome blanket of hazy fumes,

Trees veiled in a murky fog,

Trunks sombre brown with sable cracks that gnarl the bark,

All embody the ruinous ramifications of our commercialistic society.

Light barely manages to penetrate the suffocating pollution,

As we continue to blissfully disregard the biome
that's a victim of our inherent greed,

The biome without which life would cease to
thrive,

The ocean.

It unconsciously absorbs the repercussions of our
materialistic desires,

Acidifying these viridescent pools that in turn
Dissolve:
The irridescent shells,

The whipped-cream-piled-oreo-flecked shells

The knobbly, generously swooped shells

That all corrugate and cushion the inhabitant,

Crumble at the mercy of industrialisation.

As the toxins pierce through these depths,

The vibrancy of psychedelic choirs of coral

Fade yet the murky nature of the smog heightens.

The humble pastel palace yearns for

Restoration

Sympathy

Concern

Tenderness

Devotion

Appreciation

Of this exuberant carnival of our reefs

Thus, we can't afford to neglect the harnessing of these vital qualities,

Consider this the next time you succumb to convenience over consideration.

Bycatch

Calloused palms grasp the rod and reel,

Plunging the bait that triggers another casualty,

This haul could cater for the incessant demand
for fresh catch.

The dexterity and versatility are apparent in the
weaving for nets,

As he unwinds the mooring rope from the peg,

Coiling it upon the bedewed deck,

With a scheming expression

And a languished posture.

The sole concept that he engages in,

Is the objective of augmenting the viable gain

From this catch.

Proceedings of this manner that serve to

Exploit, capitalise, and triumph

By overcatching, drive the declination of species.

We are coerced into this credence

One where we have been coaxed into handling
nature's resources recklessly,

Churning out stacks of fish

day in day out,

Depleting populations beyond amelioration.

Consequently, the prolonged and extensive
essence of these deeds,

Jeopardizes ecosystems whose continuance relies

On the maintenance of these creatures.

In the absence of sustainable management,

Our fisheries confront inevitable collapse

And we reluctantly welcome an era of food crises.

Regulating these measures is no facile feat

As unsustainable harvesting,

Detrimental avidity to profit off of our marine life,

And the refusal to conform to abide by laws,

plagues the industry.

Even with the best of intentions,

This notion of "fishing down"

Activates a domino effect,

that disrupts the classical and intricate harmony

of the ocean's performance.

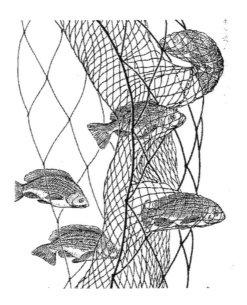

Wails

Ahead you notice a pod of barnacle encrusted humpback whales,

Breaching in the beams of dawn.

The buoyant billows of displacing water undulate,

As you relish in the jubilance of each leap and dive,

White spray erupts and expels through their blowhole.

Their streamlined backs like glaciated slates heave

Through the choppiest of shallows,

Nonetheless the essence of elegance never diminishes

As they glide, drift, flow.

Instantaneously you realise,

These moments are transient,

As you witness the remorseless souls

Hauling out these humpbacks,

Stripping them of their dignity as they lay hanging,

Confined to the meshed knots of rope that incarcerate them.

These majestic creatures are dominated by profound despondency,

Fatigue engraved on their worn faces,

And the inquisitiveness and radiance vanished.

Its family wails,

The ecosystem wails,

You wail,

Knowing that you are vulnerable against these hollow hearted slayers.

This sorrow wrenches your heart out,

Threatening to never depart,

Stealing what joy is left,

And obliterating it with their theft.

Today marks the end of this humpback's life

Yet not the end of a loss of a family

So, a mournful silence lingers in the air

As we pay tribute to another lost soul.

Irridescent spills

Flags hoisted on tanks quiver perpetually,

The tires hiss over the thick brown paste

Quenching this clay of its sandy hues

As it deposits its pernicious petroleum-based lubricants.

It accumulates whilst naturally seeping through,

Edging closer to the shore,

Every drop may seem inconsequential,

Nothing in the immensity of the ocean.

As you peer across the surface,

It seems composed, with a hint of tranquility,

Whilst concurrently deceiving you,

There's no such thing as dormancy.

Fracturing the sunlight into a mosaic of pigments,

As these toxic fluids invite themselves,

Tempted to ravage this aquatic biome.

With such an exceedingly vast volume of such
substances,

Pumped into an ecosystem that doesn't
compensate for its presence,

Overcome by a wave of helplessness,

They suppress their anguishes.

This gooey mass that forms an oil slick

Will litter the shorelines with

A hideous, hostile, repugnancy

Life will surrender to the inkiness of the tar.

Oil coats the furs of otters

And blocks the blow holes of whales,

Struck dumb by the projectile's thunder.

A sea scalded and scarred,

Its wounds tender,

As the pulsing burden of the currents

Drives the ashes of vitality.

A Dangerous Delicacy

It's early February,

Just before the lunar new year in Hong Kong,

You observe a peculiar object stuffed in various containers,

Ubiquitous - normalising this inhumanity.

The festive red bows tied around these packages

Serve to soften the blow,

Almost to solemnize and symbolise

A deep-rooted travesty.

Shark fins.

The cartilage shredded,

Texturising and thickening the glutinous broth,

A dish considered a luxury,

Embodying notions of status, hospitality and fortune.

The fins are axed,

These precious tokens that signal honour

Are ripped from its body,

As the rest is tossed apathetically,

Left to drown.

The blue shade meets its silvery flesh,

Cruising below the gentle waves,

A solemn tribute to another life at the mercy of human gluttony.

This short collection of poems strives to inspire and raise awareness for the many issues faced by our marine life and aquatic ecosystem.

Each poem focusses on a specific challenge met and how certain actions carried out by us humans as a species can be detrimental to our wildlife.

Here is a brief summary of each poem and the main idea and message that each one aims to present.

Ikizukuri:
this is essentially the preparation of sashimi from live seafood. As you escape the bustling night life, you enter a restaurant without any expectation that you'd be served with such a dish. The animation of the food in front of you indicates its freshness but you are also overcome by a sensation of repulsion and disgust as you realise what you have just partaken in.

Broken shells:
This poem deals with the drastic consequences of ocean acidification on shells and corals. Through our increased rate of burning fossil fuels, carbon

dioxide accumulates in the atmosphere, causing global warming as well as affecting our oceans. As the carbon dioxide enters our oceans, it reacts with sea water to form carbonic acid. Many creatures make chalky shells and exoskeletons for themselves out of calcium carbonate. Coral reefs will be especially devastated by ocean acidification as the rise in acidity will cause the corals to erode faster than they can grow to replace those destructed.

Bycatch:
Bycatch is the incidental capture of non target organism, that eventually lead to the decline of a species. The discarded catch of marine species and unobserved mortality due to a direct contact with fishing gear and nets. Another issue associated with bycatch includes disrupting the food chain by inadvertently taking fish or marine life that other organisms depend on to survive. For fishers, it causes conflicts and disputes among other fisheries. In conclusion, bycatch is an

extremely complex set of scientific issues that
include economic, political and moral challenges.

Wails:

Commercial whaling has been happening for
centuries, exploiting whales for profit that led to
the whole destruction of most of the world's large
species of whales. This behaviour endangers
whales and has the potential to disrupt ecosystems
and environments. We're already killing whales
indirectly daily through fishery entanglements,
military, ship strikes and seismic blasting. Due to
industrialisation and construction, we are
increasingly displacing whales leading to the
destruction of their habitats. In the current
situation, whales live in degraded oceans,
depleted and fractured populations, and are
constantly presented with human threats.

Iridescent spills:
Oil spills cause a wide range of impacts in the
marine environment and in our communities,

causing serious distress to ecosystems and to the people living near the contaminated coastline which ultimately impairs their quality of life. Oil harms all species whether it be destroying the insulating abilities of fur covered mammals, and the water repellancy of feathers which exposes creatures to extreme conditions. Without the ability to repel and insulate from the cold waters, animals will die from hypothermia. Impacts on the public include illnesses caused by toxic fumes or by ingesting contaminated fish. Preventing oil spills is of the utmost priority and this responsibility lies equally on individuals as well as on industries and countries because the source of these spills into the ocean are due to carelessness rather than it being an accident. Besides the direct harm to wildlife, these spills impoverish the people of these nations who depend on its rich body of water for food, culture, environmental and recreation.

Dangerous Delicacy:
Over the last few years, the demand for shark fins, especially for soups and traditional medicines, has

increased very rapidly. It's a dish often associated with privilege and societal rank, yet around 73million sharks are killed for this sole purpose, an indiscriminate murder that is pushing many species to the brink of exctintion. Essentially, a shark is caught, pulled onbaord to have its fins sliced off, then tossed overboard to drown or bleed to death. Not only is this an extremely wasteful and harmful practice, it's also essentially pointless since shark fins have no nutritional or medicinal value. However, this practise will continue to the point that these animals (that are so important for our ecosystem and ecological balance of our oceans) will be completely wiped out. Much of the problem that surrounds policies and laws with sharks is enforcement and implementing these regulations. Some countries simply don't have the resources to to monitor the oceans over which they have jurisdiction and to punish those who break these laws.

I hope that in reading this short collection of poems, you have become more aware of the threats that our oceans and marine life face and that you are inspired to lead a greener life, no matter how small your actions may be. Don't lose hope, because we can all make a significant change in our communities and benefit the many generations to come in preserving our natural environments.